WE'RE GOING ON A
LION HUNT

David Axtell

SQUARE
FISH

Henry Holt and Company · New York

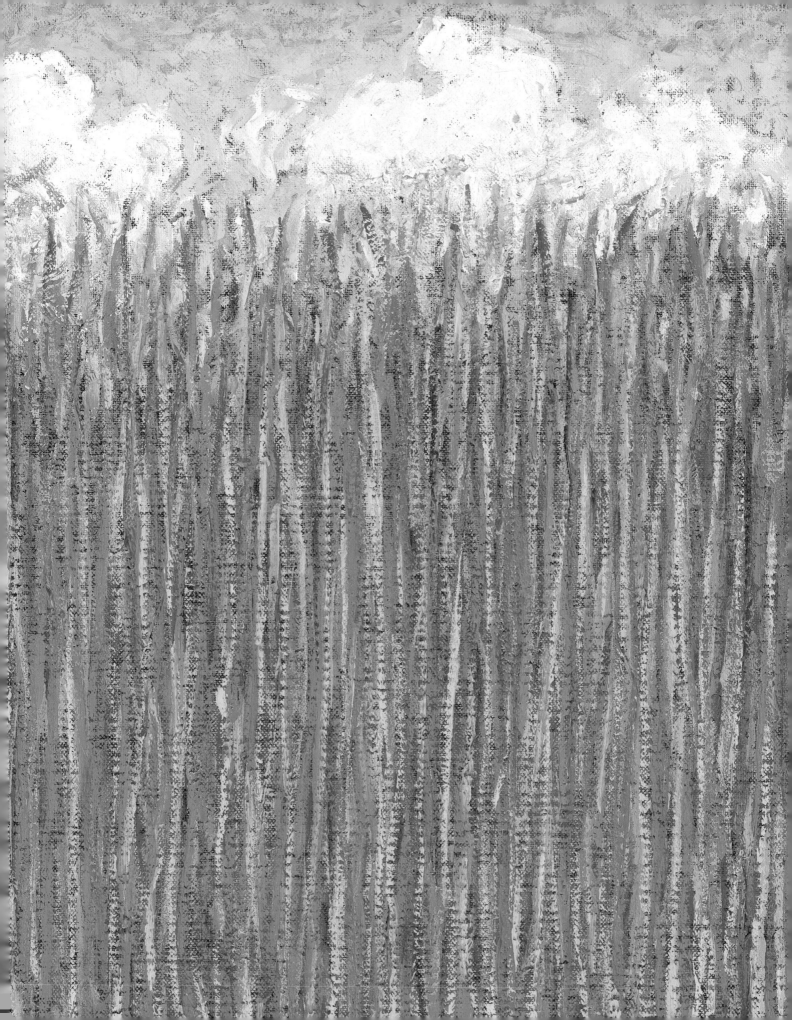

For Chantelle and Sophie

SQUARE FISH

An Imprint of Macmillan

WE'RE GOING ON A LION HUNT. Text copyright © 1999 by Macmillan Publishers Limited.
Illustrations copyright © 1999 by David Axtell. All rights reserved.
Printed in China.
For information, address Square Fish, 175 Fifth Avenue, New York, NY 10010.

Square Fish and the Square Fish logo are trademarks of Macmillan and
are used by Henry Holt and Company under license from Macmillan.

Library of Congress Cataloging-in-Publication Data
We're going on a lion hunt / illustrated by David Axtell.
p.   cm.
Summary: Two girls set out bravely in search of a lion, going through
long grass, a swamp, and a cave before they find what they're looking for.
ISBN 978-0-8050-8219-7
[1. Lions—Fiction. 2. Africa—Fiction.] I. Axtell, David, ill.
PZ7.W4712 1999   [E]—dc21   98-47507

Originally published in the United Kingdom by Macmillan Children's Books,
a division of Macmillan Publishers Limited, London.
First published in the United States by Henry Holt and Company
First Square Fish Edition: August 2012
Square Fish logo designed by Filomena Tuosto
mackids.com

7 9 10 8 6

AR: 1.1 / LEXILE: BR

We're going on a lion hunt.
We're going to catch a big one.
We're not scared.
Been there before.

We're going on a lion hunt.

We're going to catch a big one.

We're not scared.

Been there before.

Oh, no . . .

Long grass!

Can't go *over* it.

Can't go *under* it.

Can't go *around* it.

Have to go *through* it.

Swish, swash, swish, swash.

We're going on a lion hunt.

We're going to catch a big one.

We're not scared.

Been there before.

Oh, no . . .

A lake!

Can't go *over* it.

Can't go *under* it.

Can't go *around* it.

Have to go *through* it.

Splish, splash, splish, splash.

We're going on a lion hunt.

We're going to catch a big one.

We're not scared.

Been there before.

Oh, no . . .

A swamp!

Can't go *over* it.

Can't go *under* it.

Can't go *around* it.

Have to go *through* it.

Squish, squash, squish, squash.

We're going on a lion hunt.

We're going to catch a big one.

We're not scared.

Been there before.

Oh, no . . .

A Big Dark Cave!

Can't go *over* it.

Can't go *under* it.

Can't go *around* it.

Have to go *through* it.

In we go,
Tiptoe, tiptoe.

But **what's that?**

One shiny wet **nose!**

One big shaggy **mane!**

Four big furry **paws!**

It's a lion!

Back through the cave.
Back we go.

Tiptoe, tiptoe.

Back through the swamp.

Squish, squash, squish, squash.

Back through the lake.

Splish, splash, splish, splash.

Back through the long grass.

Swish, swash, swish, swash.

All the way home.

Slam the door—
CRASH!

We're all tired now.
Tired and sleepy.

Better catch a lion tomorrow instead!

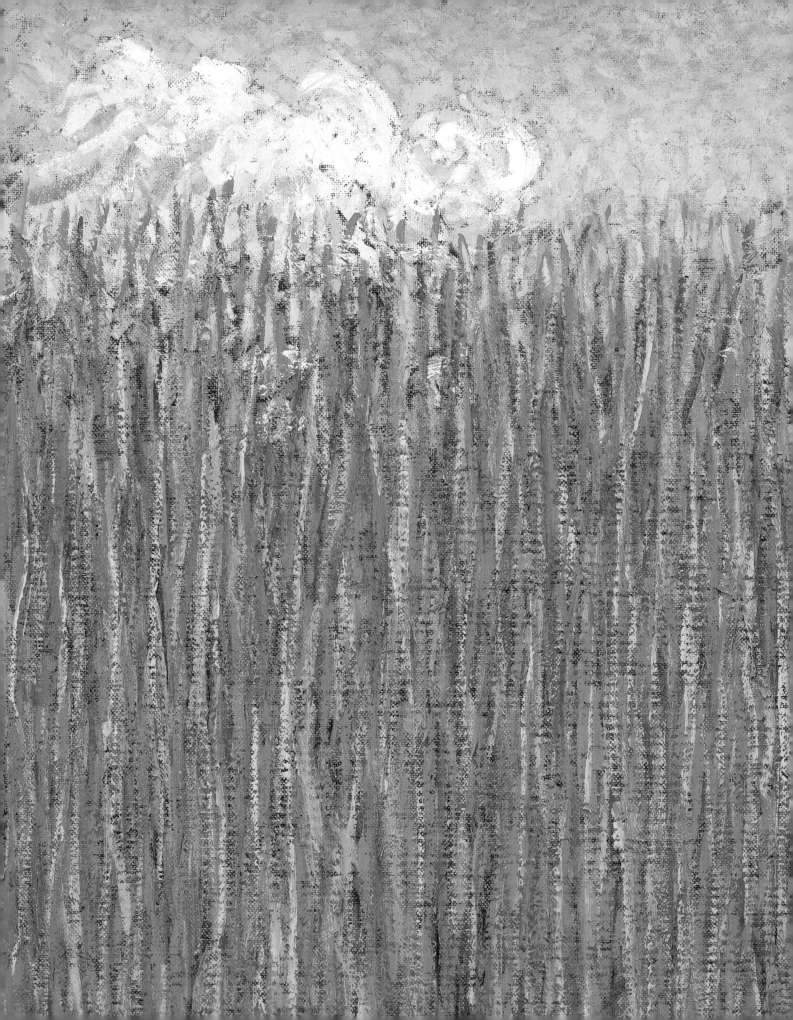